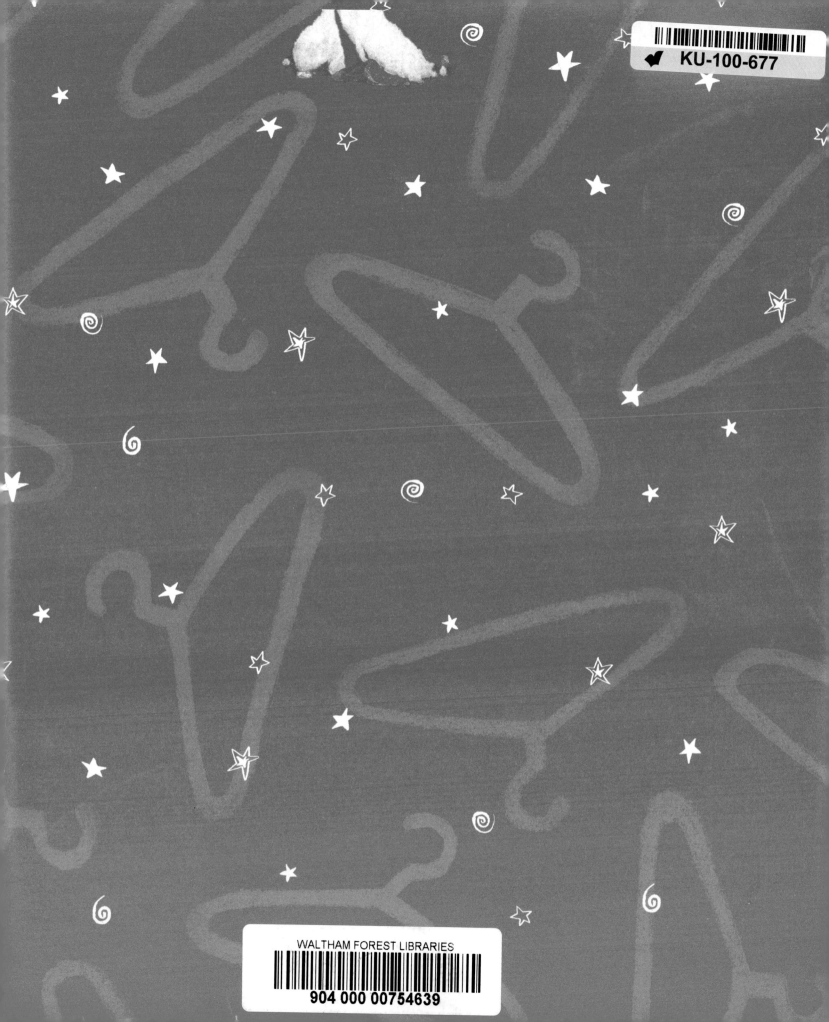

The Bear who had Nothing to Wear

A book to share from
Scallywag Press

For Archie – J.W.

First published in Great Britain in 2023
by Scallywag Press Ltd, 10 Sutherland Row, London SW1V 4JT

Text copyright © Jeanne Willis, 2023
Illustration copyright © Brian Fitzgerald, 2023
The rights of Jeanne Willis and Brian Fitzgerald have been asserted by them
in accordance with the Copyright, Designs and Patents Act, 1988

Printed on FSC paper in China by Toppan Leefung
001

British Library Cataloguing in Publication Data available
ISBN 978–1–915252–03–6

The Bear who had Nothing to Wear

WRITTEN BY
Jeanne Willis ★ Brian Fitzgerald

ILLUSTRATED BY

Scallywag Press Ltd
LONDON

There once was a bear who had NOTHING to wear,
And normally, teddy bears don't really care,
They're happy to dress how you want them to dress
But Albie was *not*, I am bound to confess.

Albie arrived wearing nothing but fur,
He could have been either a Him or a Her.
Most teddy bears let their owner decide . . .

But Albie would NOT,
for a bear has its pride.

Was Albie a daddy bear, mummy or baby?
When asked, he would growl a grumbly 'Maybe'
For sometimes he wasn't –
and sometimes he was!

Which made choosing his costumes a problem because . . .

On MONDAY, he dressed like an infant all day.

Then . . .

. . . he pulled off his bonnet
and threw it away!

He kicked his blue bootees
right out of the pram,

'Wrong outfit!' he shouted,
'That's *not* who I am!'

'Today I'm a **prince**, so I need a **gold crown** . . .

... Pantaloons and a tunic, a ruby red gown.

And unicorn slippers and gloves if you please.'

But...

. . . On TUESDAY, he screamed,
'I am *not* wearing these!'

'I'm a Fairy Queen Bear – I need glittery wings!
And a wand and a dress made of petals and things

And dancing shoes, then I can
go to the ball . . .'

But sadly, the Fairy King Bear didn't call.

Albie threw his new clothes
in the back of a drawer.

'It's WEDNESDAY,' he said,
'I must order some more,

I need cowboy boots, spurs
and a ten-gallon hat . . .

I'm a Cowboy – Yee-ha! I look splendid like that.'

And he did – but . . .

... On THURSDAY, he fell off his horse,
Yelling 'Cowboy Bear? Poo ...

I'm a *pirate*, of course!

I need breeches,
a frilly white shirt
and a hook

And a wig and an eyepatch
to capture the look.'

He sailed the high seas but he wasn't too keen.

And by FRIDAY, poor Albie felt seasick and green.

So . . .

He bundled his pirate gear under the bed . . .

And decided to dress for the city instead.
He bought shiny shoes and a suit and a coat . . .

But he hated the train ride as much as the boat.

He felt sticky and icky and sweaty and hot,
And cried, 'Am I a City Bear? No, I am NOT!'

'I'm a **Country Bear** now,
so I need a tweed cap

And a jacket with pockets
that close with a flap

And some wellingtons – Yes!
I look **perfect** in these.'

But . . .

He sank in a cowpat right up to his knees.
He was teased by a weasel and taunted by crows

And regretted the SATURDAY outfit he chose,

So . . .

He stripped to his fur and he skipped through the wood
And the breeze on his knees felt exceedingly good

And as bare as a teddy can possibly be,
He felt free and he sang,

'This is me! This is me!'

So on SUNDAY he put all his clothes into bags.

And gave them away to poor
teddies in rags.

And apart from a hat in his favourite style,
All he wears now is . . .

A beautiful smile!